Stories of the Supernatural
By Mark Wilkins
A Storyteller Series Book

Table of Contents

Preface

This book is a combination of two books called Stories of The Supernatural 1 & 2.

I have always loved hearing supernatural stories, which include ghost stories, horror stories, stories about monsters and about death incarnate. This book is filled with a lot of stories. Some are long and some are short. Some are even in rhyme. There is something in this book for everyone who is a fan of any of these genres and even for those who aren't. If you want to hear about how I created some of these stories, there is a series of videos by my publisher called On Creating where different authors, including myself, tell about how they came to write various stories or books. If you are interested in knowing about the creative process type Love Force International Publishing onto you tube and you should get the channel. I also have some excerpts of this on my blog Mark Wilkins Author on the Word Press blogging platform. Please follow me on kindle. You can get information on my latest releases, etc.

The Longest Hangover

She got out of bed with a splitting headache. Her vision was blurry. A red haze filtered everything she could see. That must've been one hell of a party she went to last night. She had been an alcoholic for so many years that she didn't really remember the party or how she got back home but she felt the pain of a hangover pounding inside her head like a disco.

She looked around the room. The dresser was still there. The mirror hanging over the dresser wasn't cracked. There weren't champagne glasses or beer cans strewn about the floor. She didn't see any used condoms strewn about. Good. At least the party didn't take place in her bedroom.

Then she glanced over to her desk. Her laptop was there and it was on. Fighting the blistering pain of a headache, she squinted and stared at it hard, trying to make out what it was on. It was on her Facebook page. How odd, she thought.

She stumbled over to her desk. She became very dizzy. She plopped down in the plush leather chair next to her desk. She stared at the computer screen. It looked like her Facebook Page. Her name was on it and all of the interfaces were there. Something however, was very wrong with it. After a few more minutes of staring at the screen, she realized what it was. All of her 650 Facebook friends had disappeared!

Then her concentration was broken by the unmistakable sound of an instant message. She stared at the screen. A message appeared. It said: "Hi, I think I knew you in High School, I think we used to chat a lot. I even came over your house once." Barry.

She read the message and tried to remember if she knew anyone named Barry. That name wasn't familiar. She was about to IM him back to tell him he had contacted the wrong person but she gave his IM one last look. This time the words "High School" stuck out. High School, she thought, did I know a Barry in High School? She thought about it for a few minutes.

Then she remembered. Yeah, there was a Barry. He seemed to like her. He was shy and kind of cute. They did chat sometimes. He may have come to her house once or twice. Oh, but then he got involved with heavy drugs. It wasn't long after that that he disappeared from her social scene and a few weeks after that he disappeared completely. She recalls one of her friends repeating a rumor about him, what was it...oh, yeah, he witnessed a murder and was supposedly on the run. Anyway, no one ever saw or heard from him again. Could he have left town and returned again all these years later? She responded to Barry's IM: "Send me a friend request."

A couple of minutes later, she noticed a friend request, saw it was from Barry and she approved it. She IM'd Barry.

"What ever happened to you?" she texted. "I heard a rumor that you witnessed a murder. Did you leave town?" She continued.

"I had to." He replied. "But I'm here now." He continued.

Just then, she got another IM. It was from Billy. Billy was her boyfriend after she graduated high school. He went into the Army.

"Billy?" She replied.

"It's me." He responded.

Those two words hit her like a bullet to the heart. She froze and began weeping inconsolably. She collected her composure. Her thin, fragile fingers trembled as she texted him back.

"I heard you were killed in the Middle East." She wrote.

"No. He Replied. "I was lost in the Middle East but I found myself here." He Continued.

As she read the words, she figured that he must have been evacuated in a medical helicopter and sent to a hospital. Perhaps he lost a limb or was blind and felt awkward about contacting her. Poor Billy, she thought. Thinking about him was more than she could bear.

"My mom is calling." She texted. "I've gotta go. Take care." She Continued.

She felt guilty using her mother as an excuse. She knew that she hadn't talked to Billy in about 10 years and she knew there was no way he knew that her mother had died three years ago. As she stared at the computer screen, her mind began wandering and she started remembering the good times she and Billy shared. Soon, she was completely lost in her memories of Billy. She sat there, waxing nostalgic for what seemed to be hours. Then she looked up. There were 35 new friend requests on her Facebook page!

She began to look down the list. There were people she used to work with. Some classmates from high school and college. She got one from a teacher she had in elementary school. She even got one from her old postman and a guy she dated back when she was 22.
She wondered why she was suddenly hearing from all of these people she hadn't talked to in years. The more she thought about it, the more it made her want to find her current friends, the 650 friends who suddenly disappeared. She was about to shut down her computer and reboot it in hopes of getting them back but was stopped by the sound of a new IM. She was compelled to look at it. It was from her mother.

She clicked it open it read: "Welcome home dear. Mother."

As she read it, she felt dizzy and sick. She turned, got up and stumbled towards her bed. As she got closer, she saw that someone was already lying in her bed! Then she remembered. There was no party last night. There was no hangover. She went to bed with a bad headache. She must have died in her sleep. She realized that all of the new friends on her Facebook must have died as well.

Jimmy

Brad had a bad week. He lost his best friend and neighbor. It was Brad's first day at school and his best friend Rob walked with him to school. Rob was a year older and knew the way. Brad followed along with Rob on the way to school. By the time the school day was over, Brad thought he knew the way, even though he hadn't ever walked to school before. He insisted that they walk down a particular street. Rob, even though he knew the way, had a weaker will and he let Brad convince him to go down that street. Four hours and a ride in a police car later, Brad was proven wrong.

After walking four miles in the wrong direction, the two came upon a policeman who gave them a ride home when they told him they were lost. It was a good thing Rob knew his address because Brad had been living in this foster home for just two months and he had no idea what the address was. The policeman actually knew who the two boys were because their parents had called the police station and reported them missing after they were two hours late.

When they arrived home, both Rob's parents and Brad's foster parents were relieved. Brad's foster parents were just happy he was alive but Rob's dad was very angry. He told Brad to never come to their house again. He told Rob to never play with Brad again and to never even talk to him. He gave Rob one last directive: Under no circumstances was he to ever walk to or from school with Brad again.

For the next week, Brad's foster mother first had Brad follow her car as she drove slowly to and from his school. Then, followed him to and from school to insure that he knew the route. He spent half the day the next Saturday walking to and from school five times. He went to bed early that night, not because he was being punished but because he was tired.

The following week, Brad walked to school by himself. Rob made sure to leave long before Brad did so he could avoid the awkwardness of having to see him on the street. Despite the fact that they were in different classes, Brad would see Rob at school every day during lunch. He tried to wave hello to Rob once but Rob just looked in the other direction.

The Father of one of the kids in Brad's class worked for the police department. He told his son the story of the two lost boys. That boy told other kids in Brad's class. Soon Brad was known as "The Lost Boy". The other kids in the school shunned him after that.

For the next few weeks, Brad walked to school by himself. He ate lunch by himself. He went home and sat by himself. He had no friends. The other kids wouldn't even talk to him except to call him Lost Boy.

Then, one day, he was walking to school. He was feeling particularly sad and lonely. As he passed Church Street, which was about half way on his trip, he heard someone walking behind him. Frightened, he walked a little faster. The footsteps behind him began walking faster. Brad made a fist and turned around quickly ready to hit someone. As he turned around, he saw a boy his age, dressed in faded blue denim overalls.

"Are you following me?" Brad Asked.

"No," Said the Boy. I am just going to school."

"Oh," replied Brad.

"Can I walk with you?" The boy asked.

"Sure." Said Brad.

"My name is Jimmy." Said the boy.

"I'm Brad." Brad Replied.

They walked a few blocks in silence. Then Jimmy began to talk.

"I'm sort of new here." Said Jimmy. "Can you show me around? Everything is so different from what I am used to." He continued.

Brad looked over Jimmy's clothing. His faded denim overalls and hard black shoes looked dated. He was going to say something to Jimmy about it but he didn't want to be rude. He didn't want to blow a chance at having at least one friend.

"I'm sort of new here myself." Brad replied. "But sure, I can show you." He continued.

They continued walking. When Brad and Jimmy got to school, Brad showed Jimmy around.

"What Teacher do you have?" Jimmy asked.

"Old Lady Hubbard." Replied Brad.

"Where I went to school there was a Miss Hubbard but she was young and pretty and every boy had a crush on her." Jimmy said reminiscing.

"Well, our Miss Hubbard has been teaching here for 43 years. It's hard to believe that anyone in their right mind would have a crush on her." Replied Brad.

Brad and Jimmy spent the whole day together. While Brad gave Jimmy his opinions about many of the students in his class he never introduced Jimmy to them because he didn't really know him that well and they didn't really talk to him.

They walked together after school. When they reached Church Street, Jimmy said goodbye and walked up the street. Brad kept on walking home. When Brad got home, he told his foster mother all about his new friend. He was so excited to have a friend. When she told him about his clothes, she told him that perhaps he was poor and that he shouldn't ever ask him about his clothing because it might embarrass him. Brad couldn't wait to go to school the next day.

For the next month, Brad and Jimmy walked to and from school together every day. Every day, without fail, Jimmy was waiting for Brad on the corner of Church Street. Every day, Jimmy sat next to Brad in class, sat next to him during lunch and next to him during Physical Education period.

Lunch time and Physical Education period gave them a lot of time to talk. Jimmy never ate lunch. He always said he had a big breakfast. So he just sat and talked. During Physical Education period no one ever picked Lost Boy Brad for their team so he spent a lot of time on the bench talking to Jimmy.

Brad told Jimmy about his foster home. He told him about Rob and the fun they used to have playing. He told Jimmy about the time they got lost and what Rob's father had said. Jimmy told Brad about his life. He said that he didn't have a computer or a cell phone at his house. He said his mother always called him her "Little Angel". She said he was sent from heaven to bring joy to the world. Brad liked the way Jimmy pronounced the word often. All the other kids pronounced it often but Jimmy pronounced it "Off Ten".

One day, during Physical Education period, while Brad and Jimmy were sitting on the bench yacking away, Brad's classmates were picking team members for a game of baseball. They realized they were short one player. One of Brad's Team mates yelled over to Brad.

"Hey, Lost Boy!" He shouted.

Brad ignored him. He shouted again.

"Hey, Lost Boy! Brad! You want to play on our team? "He shouted.
"Can Jimmy play too?" Brad Replied.
"Who?" responded the puzzled boy dumbfounded.
"Jimmy!" Brad said as he turned to look at Jimmy. Jimmy wasn't there!

Brad looked towards the bungalow where his class was. He saw Jimmy running towards it. Brad took off after him. Jimmy ran past the bungalow and towards the main building. Brad followed about 50 yards behind him. Jimmy ran past the main building, jumped the fence and ran out onto the street. Brad followed. Jimmy ran three more blocks and Brad fell behind. After another couple of blocks, Brad was 100 yards behind Jimmy. All the time he ran, he kept yelling for Jimmy to come back. Jimmy never stopped.

Then Jimmy turned down Church Street. Brad followed huffing and puffing about 75 yards behind him. Then Brad turned up Church Street. He couldn't see any houses, just high shrubbery. He ran up two blocks and heard a metal gate closing. He ran to the gate and entered what he thought was somebody's garden. He was surprised to see he was in a cemetery.

Suddenly, he saw Jimmy running across some grave. He began running after him. Jimmy ran behind a tree and disappeared. Brad thought perhaps Jimmy was hiding behind the tree. He thought perhaps Jimmy was very upset or emotional. So he began walking slowly towards it. "Jimmy, why did you run away?" He said. It'll be okay, you can talk to me." He concluded.

When he got to the tree Brad peeked behind it. No one was there. Then, the glint of the sun off of something metallic just a few graves down caught his eye. He walked over to the grave. It had a headstone with a metal frame embedded in it. The glass in the frame was dirty. Brad wiped if off with his shirt sleeve. He saw an old photograph of a little boy in overalls. The headstone read:
Jimmy Apple
"Our Little Angel"
Rest in Peace

Brad stood there and cried. He was sad for this boy who had died some thirty eight years before. He was sad that a little boy had to die and sad because he knew his friend would never come back.

He didn't go back to school for a few days. When he did, he arrived early and asked Miss Hubbard if she knew a boy named Jimmy Apple. With a tear in her eye, she told him she did. Then she got a scrap book from her desk drawer. There were photos and letters and newspaper clippings about her past students. Some became big business people. Others became doctors or teachers like her. One became a judge and another was on the City Council.

Then she turned to a page in the back of the book. There was a lone newspaper clipping. The headline read "Lost Boy Found". It told the story of a little boy named Jimmy Apple who had gotten lost on a camping trip in a forested area. It talked about an extensive search, a year-long mystery and how his skeletal remains were found at the bottom of a 300 foot high ravine a little past a year after he went missing.

"Jimmy Apple was my student not long after I began teaching here. " Miss Hubbard said.

"Although the other students don't remember him and the school has long since forgotten about him, I will never forget him. I think of him often" She continued.

"You mean Off Ten." Brad replied.

A startled look came over old Miss Hubbard's face, then, momentarily it settled into a glow, that made her eyes appear to have the twinkle of youth. "Yes, Off Ten." She said reminiscing. "It's so strange, you say it just like he did so many years ago. Are you related to him?" She asked.

"Kind of," Said Brad. "I was lost once too but I think I've found my way now."

Death and I

Death visited me
Though he only stayed a short while
He didn't linger
Nor did he take me with him
I found his company to be quite pleasant
Liberating actually
He promised to return again one day
And take me with him
In the years that have passed since
I have seen him visiting
Friends and relatives and neighbors
He takes them with him
Sometimes our eyes meet
And we nod at one another
In a respectful manner
Like those who are acquainted with one another
I know one day he will return
To take me away with him
But I am not afraid
I am familiar with death
And know that there is nothing to fear about him

A Lump of Coal

Herman Braun was a self-made man. At least, that's what the public perception was. Born the year that World War One began, Braun's rise matched the rise of Europe itself. The truth was, Herman Braun began life as Albert Schnizzel. The son of a wealthy shipping tycoon. His father owned a fleet of 150 oil tankers. He moved oil across the globe and made handsome profits doing so.

Albert was the apple of his mother's eye. She bought him everything he wanted. She let him eat whatever he wanted. At nine he was a plump little piglet with a pig like nose and fat features. Albert's parents were killed in a car accident when their car lost control going down the mountain that their mansion, Eagles Nest sat atop of. Nine year old Albert was sent to live with the family of his mother's brother, the middle class train conductor, Balthezar Goonabi.

His first Christmas in the Goonabi household proved to be bleak. Instead of getting the kind of toys his mother used to shower him with, he got a lone lump of coal in his Christmas stocking. Although the Goonabi's claimed that they had put a present in his stocking and they had no idea who could have replaced their present with coal, Albert knew they had done it out of spite for who he really was, a future millionaire.

Albert got up and left the house before dawn to go on the 3 mile walk to his school. On his way, he passed merchants opening up their stores, delivery men, street venders and homeless people. He knew everyone's face because he passed them five days a week. As he passed near the meat market, he saw a strange old man lying in the gutter. He was tall, skinny, bald and had a long, scraggly beard. He was dressed in work pants and a white tee shirt, blackened by dirt, grime and soot. As he approached, the man said "I know what you did!" Albert noticed that the man had rotten teeth.

Albert tried to walk passed the man quickly, but as he passed, the man grabbed his ankle. Albert froze in horror. The Man spoke.

"I know what you did and that's why you got a lump of coal in your stocking." He said in a craggy voice.

Too afraid to look down at the man, Albert tried to kick himself free but the more he kicked, the more the man held firm.

"Years from now, you will get another lump of coal for Christmas and when you do, I'll come for you." He said.

Albert tried to kick his way to freedom even harder. He started to scream. People on the street came running over to him.

"What's wrong lad? "A man said.

"That ugly old man won't let me go!" Albert replied.

"What old man?" the man asked.

Albert looked down only to see that his foot was caught in an overgrown weed.

His face grew red with embarrassment as looked at the man. He kicked himself loose from the weed and broke into a run. As he ran, the wind began whistling in his ear. He swore he heard the old man's voice saying "I'll be coming for youuuuuu!"

Albert wondered what he had seen and felt. Was it real? Was it an illusion? He wasn't sure. And how did whatever that was know his secret? Was it really the one who put the lump of coal in his stocking or was it a reflection of his guilty conscience?

The fear he felt wasn't because the old man was a stranger. It wasn't because the old man grabbed his ankle. It was because the old man seemed to know his secret. It was a secret that he had kept hidden for months and would keep hidden for years. He had killed his parents.

Since a young age Albert was always fascinated with machines and how they worked. When he was just four years old, his father took him on a tour of one of his oil tankers. When they went to the engine room, Albert sat spellbound watching the engine work. Soon, instead of asking for the type of toys other children asked for, Albert asked for small machines. He took the machines apart and then put them back together again.

When he was six, Albert began watching his father's mechanic work on his father's cars. He helped out, sometimes, handing the man tools. By the time he was eight, he could take a car engine apart and put it back together again.

Albert became so absorbed with machines that he let his studies lag. His father locked him in his room each night until he did his homework. By the time he was finished, his father's mechanic had gone home. Hating that he was kept away from machines, Albert snuck out of his room one night went to his father's garage and cut the brake line on the car his father was supposed to take on a business trip the next day. When his father decided to use it later that night to take Albert's mother to a play, they both died in the accident that resulted from Albert's foul play.

Albert suffered through years of being bullied in middle class schools while his father's company was run by its Board of Directors. He went to a public college and majored in finance. When Albert turned 21, he inherited the company. It had been run well and doubled in size and power within the tanker industry. Albert didn't want to be in the Oil Tanker business, so he immediately sold the company to its Board of Directors for a billion dollars, much less than it was worth.

Fearing that people would try to steal the money from him, Albert went into hiding for three years under the name of Heinrich Bulger. During this time he traveled the world non-stop enjoying the best amenities each continent could offer. Heinrich sewed his oats, had fun and broke many a girl's heart.

He emerged in Vienna in 1938 as a wealthy art dealer Franz Frunk. He made a killing buying and selling art stolen by the Nazi's. As World War 2 drew to a close, he got bored of that and reemerged in Switzerland as inventor Karl Loganfuhr. He created custom built cars that had some innovations that were years ahead of their time. Loganfuhr built the cars himself and although it was a joy, it took too much of his time and he quit between cars 35 and 36.

Herman Braun emerged in Belgium in the mid-1950s as a real estate developer and contractor. He built commercial and rental properties throughout Europe. He was notorious for paying off public officials to move the poor from prime real estate and then buying and re-building an entire neighborhood making it attractive to upper middle class families. He never gave a second thought about what happened to the people he displaced.

It was at this time that he married and had children. Not so much out of love or desire for family but as a duty to prolong his legacy. He had 6 children, all of them males. Albert, the oldest was born in 1957. Herman, was born in 1961. Twins Karl and Carl were born in 1965. Franz was born in 1971 and Heinrich, the youngest was born in 1975. Herman trained every one of them in the business. As he expanded, he put a different one in charge of a different section of the globe.

By the 1970's Braun's company had extended its powerful tentacles into the Middle East and Africa. By the 1980's Braun International added choice properties in Asia to its portfolio. By the 1990's South America and Australia fell under its grip. By 2000, America was swayed into submission with the increased value of the Euro. In 1980, Albert and Herman were given control of Braun International operations in Europe and Asia. In 1989 the twins were given control of South America, Africa and the Middle East. In 1993 Franz was given control of Australia. In 2000, Heinrich was given control of operations in North America.

By 2017, 103 year old Herman Braun was still in semi-retirement. His face was wrinkled, his body was withered but his mind was still sharp and his vision for Braun International was clear. He still had a say in global operations and planning. He left his sons to do the execution.

By this time his sons had all married and had children. Some even had grand-children. In 2016 he bought & refurbished Eagles Nest, his childhood home. In November 2017, he moved in. He called his entire family up to Eagle's Nest for a family Christmas. Despite a storm, they all came to spend Christmas with Herman.

On Christmas Eve, after a grand feast prepared by Herman's cooking staff, the family settled down to opening their gifts. Herman's great-grandchildren were showered with toys and electronic devices of all types. His grand-children were all given sports cars. His sons and their wives all got black cards with ten million dollar spending limits on them.

Herman himself received all kinds of gifts, from an Iphone, to a new laptop computer, to a cashmere bathrobe and slippers, which he immediately put on. His favorite great-granddaughter, six year old Murtha, gave him a hand drawn picture of Santa Claus with the words "You are the Santa in all of our lives." The drawing really touched the faint remainder of what was young Albert's-old Herman's heart. Then he saw a crudely wrapped little present. He looked at Murtha.
"Is it from you?" he asked.

Murtha shook her head indicating "no". He gave her a doubting smile as he unwrapped the package. Then, he opened it. He fell back with a horrified look on his face. He dropped the gift. It was a lone lump of coal. He knew what the gift meant and unlike when he was nine years old, he had, through research, come to know where it came from.

Then, the elderly man leaned back in his easy chair as he began to speak. His forehead furrowed as he raised his left eye brow.
"There is a story behind this gift." He said. Then he told the story.

It began long ago, in what today is known as The Netherlands but back then was called Holland. It began with twin brothers, different as night and day. When they were younger, you couldn't tell them apart physically but as they grew older the differences in their character began to manifest as differences in their physical appearance.

Kris grew up to be tall and slender but amazingly strong. He had pleasant features to match his disposition. He always had a kind word for everyone and went out of his way to help the poor, the invalid and the afflicted. In his youth he worked for the Dutch East India Company. He traveled all across the world finding things that might be of interest to Europeans looking for something different or unique to spice up their dreary lives.

Kris became successful. He was considered an asset to the company and was rewarded handsomely making him instantly wealthy. He opened up a gift shop and negotiated a deal with the Dutch East India Company to allow him to get a percentage of the things he discovered in lieu of a salary. His gift shop became the most popular in Europe causing him to open another and then another. Soon he had 40 gift shops, having at least one in every major city in Europe.

Kris' twin brother Jack grew up to be overweight with cruelly twisted and distorted facial features. This matched his disposition for he himself had a cruel streak. His disliked most people and enjoyed seeing small animals and even people suffering. Jack heard voices and saw people who weren't really there. In our day we call people like this schizophrenic.

Kris loved his brother and he in fact, felt sorry for him. Jack was too ill tempered to hold down any kind of job so Kris got him hired by the Dutch East India Company. Jack too became good at procuring things for The Company but where Kris procured them through win / win negotiations, Jack procured them through nefarious means.

Like Kris, Jack became an asset to the Dutch East India Company. Like Kris, Jack was rewarded handsomely and like Kris, Jack saved his money. Jack used his money to purchase illegal contraband which he in turn sold to people who were desperate to obtain it. He procured opium for a criminal cartel in Marseilles, France. He supplied gun powder to a War Lord in West Africa. He secured guns and cannon for despots across the globe. The blood of countless thousands was on his hands but all he could see were the profits.

Their lives ran their course and they both became very successful. As they both prospered they both attracted a different crowd of people. Kris became a Deacon in his church and a pillar of his community. He donated huge sums to charity and went to the poor sections of different communities every Christmas and gave away gifts to the children. People even began to write to him stating what kind of gift their child wanted and Kris always made sure someone showed up at their doorstep on Christmas with their custom gift. When Kris died, at the age of 68, ten thousand people attended his funeral.

Jack, on the other hand, attracted a rough crowd of vagabonds, scoundrels and thieves. He used them and needed them in his business affairs. They became his friends. The richer he got, the greedier they became. They eventually swindled him out of his entire life savings. He died of syphilis, and starvation in the gutter of a dark and dingy street in a European city at the age of 47. His emaciated skeleton like body was dumped into a pauper's grave.

Just as the brothers took separate paths in life, so did they take separate paths in death. Touched by his giving life and good works, God resurrected Kris and sent him to the North Pole. Appearing as he had at the height of his life, he would appear in royal robes of red and deliver presents not only to poor children but to good children all over the world.

Intrigued by all of his evil deeds, Satan had plans for Jack. Every Christmas, Jack, dressed and appearing as he did on the day he died, was sent to visit the horrible children, the ones that did something so bad, they couldn't be forgiven. He would put a lump of coal in their Christmas stocking and, at some point in the future, he would return to take their life and their soul home to Satan.

"I got my first lump of coal in this very room when I was six." The old man said. "I changed my name and identity several times in my life and I guess he could never find me but I'm here now and I know he's coming for me." He continued.
"But whatever could you have done grandpapa?" asked Murtha.

Before he could answer A bolt of lightning struck the chimney and the lights went out. The entire family heard the man they knew as Herman Braun let out a bloodcurdling scream as they heard a rumbling in the Chimney. Then the lights came on. Herman had vanished. The only evidence of him having been there was a pair of slippers strewn about near the chimney. Heinrich looked up the chimney only to be pelted by drops of blood. Soon a waterfall of blood cascaded down the chimney and onto the floor.

Somewhere in Hell, Satan welcomed his newest acquisition.

Reaper Blues

CHORUS
They call me the reaper
I make them reap just what they sew
They call me the reaper
I make them reap just what they sew
It ain't easy being The Reaper
Or knowing all the things he knows

VERSE 1
He looks into the darkness
That's in the hearts of men
Knows all their dirty secrets
And all the things they did

He journeys through their darkness
And works to set things right
They try to run away
But never escape
As he banishes them into the night

They call him The Reaper

VERSE 2

I remember Miss Sally
She married a wealthy man
Never wanted to help anyone
She treated folks like trash
That was many years ago
Sally got feeble and got old
Her husband left
She had no friends
She died broke and alone
They call him The Reaper

VERSE 3
Let me tell you about Mr. Jimmy
He traveled all around
Had him a different woman
In every part of town
One thing about Mr. Jimmy
He had him a jealous wife
His cheating heart
Was torn apart
When her shotgun took his life
They call him The Reaper

A Ghost in The House

Juan and Jose were brothers. Juan was nine years old and Jose, his younger brother was five. On the night before Halloween, After he put Jose to bed, Juan he went to the kitchen and worked to Embellish his shoes with scary symbols so he could wear them as part of his Zombie costume at the Halloween Dress Up contest in school the next day. Juan bought a package of spooky stickers at the stationary shop the day before.

Juan glanced at his shoes. He smiled because he thought the shoes looked especially fresh. His thoughts were broken by a sound, "Booooo!" howled down the hallway. Juan stared down the hallway but he couldn't see anything. After a minute, he went back to staring at his shoes.

"Boooooooo!!!!" Came a howling, this time right outside of the kitchen. This time Juan stopped what he was doing and walked over to the threshold of the kitchen to investigate where the sound was coming from. He didn't see anything suspicious. He started to get a little bit scared.

He walked over to the sink and filled a cup with cold water. Then a sound came from right behind him. "BBOOOOOOOOOOOOOOOOOOOOOOO!!!!" Juan turned around suddenly and saw Part of the fabric of Jose's pajamas in a lower cabinet with, the door slightly ajar. Juan found the solution to the puzzle of who or what was making the boo sounds. He decided to negotiate with the "Ghost".

"Whoever is making those sounds…I'll give you a candy bar if you stop." He said.

Then all was silent. Two minutes passed. Then Jose opened the cabinet door and stepped out. "I Booed you." He said, adding the suffix ed to the word boo. "Now can I get my candy?' Jose asked.
"Sure," said Juan.
And the boys sat together eating the candy bar.

Cannibal Money

Hal had a great day so far. He netted a total of $63,000 in three hours. A grafter by trade, he made a living with the art of the scam. He just got three senior citizens to part with their money using an investment scheme which would return five dollars for every dollar invested within three months.

He sold them Private Stock "Preferred" Shares in the Cacamente Gold Mines of Peru. The richest new discovery of gold in the past 50 years. He had previously put up a fake internet site and meta tagged the hell out of it to insure that anyone investigating it would get his scam site, fake information and phony glowing testimonials from fictitious seniors who had invested their life savings and were millionaires as a result. Needless to say there were no Cacamente mines.

He didn't pitch any truly wealthy seniors. They vetted all potential investments through attorneys and private detectives. Either of whom could easily discover that Hal's investments were worthless. Hal had resigned himself to being stuck with middle class retirees. People who often had less than $25,000 to invest. Today, he got $35,000 from a woman in Florida, $12,000 from a man in Colorado and $16,000 from a pig farmer in Arkansas. This, together with the money he made so far this month, brought his monthly totals to $331,500.

Hal had gotten used to living well. He was a regular money cannibal, gobbling up the life savings of unsuspecting seniors. He spent money like it was water, because, as far as he was concerned, it was. He had come to realize that he was like a faucet and the endless supply of gullible seniors kept money flowing into his various bank accounts. He had a 3 million dollar townhouse on the 27th floor of a prominent building in uptown Manhattan, a two million dollar estate in Vermont and a two million dollar home in Southern California. He drove a Porsche around town, a Tesla when he wanted to impress someone who was environmentally conscious and a Lamborghini when he wanted to flaunt his wealth. Everything was bought on credit or mortgaged. He often spent beyond his means because he knew he would never have a problem keeping up with the payments.

Hal lived the lifestyle of someone who was extraordinarily wealthy. He dated actresses and fashion models and was a fixture of the night scene wherever he happened to be living at the time. He was a world traveler and kept apartments in London, Paris and Tokyo. He dined at the finest restaurants and stayed at five star hotels. He had relationships with people but never let anyone get close to him. He had many acquaintances but no true friends. When people asked what he did for a living he just told them he was an investment broker. He never let anyone he knew invest in his schemes. He didn't want anyone to connect him with his illegal businesses. Periodic changing of websites and scams made it harder for the authorities to find him, let alone prosecute him.

Hal's life wasn't always so glamorous. Back in high school he was called by his birth name, Harold. He was overweight, wore horn rimmed glasses and dressed like a fugitive from the Salvation Army Thrift Store. Girls laughed at him and guys picked on him. In the social hierarchy that dominates high schools, he was put on the bottom, in the loser category. He had no friends, no future and no joy in his life. He was smart though and his grades got him a college scholarship.

Once in college, Harold began to transform himself. He decided he wanted to lose weight. He worked out like a mad man. In two years he dropped 80 pounds. The next year, he got contact lessons. The fourth year, he took a course on etiquette. He emerged from college a handsome, well-mannered young man named Hal with a double degree in Economics and Literature. Girls were interested in him but finding a job was difficult. He got a day job to pay the bills but it didn't pay much. He had a small apartment and was in danger of being evicted when he decided to use his knowledge of Economics and internet savvy to create income.

Hal created fake companies that sounded and seemed legitimate. He bought investor lists from list brokers and began cold calling. He began making small amounts of money, an extra hundred or two a week. As the months progressed and Hal honed his ability to sell to strangers over the phone, he started making even more money. After his first two years he was making forty thousand a year extra.

Hal analyzed who his best customers were. He found that senior citizens were most likely to buy what he was selling. Many of them didn't have much internet savvy and couldn't research beyond googling the name of the company. They didn't have anyone to discuss the merit of investments with. Hal decided to concentrate on seniors exclusively. Once he did, he started making big money.

As the years progressed, so did the number of internet sites and schemes. He developed ten separate sets of bank accounts to funnel his money into. Hal knew he was playing a dangerous game and that at any moment his money could be seized by the government if he was caught plying his trade. He figured if he separated his money nobody could get a hold of more than one or two of the accounts and he would have money to fight or for flight if he needed to get out of the country.

By the time he went to his ten year high school reunion, Hal was well established and was gobbling up and spitting out cash like a broken ATM. Hal literally surprised all of his former classmates. The guys who used to pick on him wanted to be him. The girls who made fun of him wanted to have his baby. He could have made some lifelong connections from the reunion but Hal had long since moved beyond his former oppressors. He didn't want any of them as friends and he didn't want any of them to discover how he made his money.

Hal was suddenly hungry. He was about to break for lunch but didn't want to break the mojo of his morning hot streak. He decided to make one more call. He looked down at the next name on the list. Ignatius M. Karma, 97, New Orleans, Louisiana. He dialed the number. After three rings someone picked up.

"Hello." Said the voice on the other end.

"Is this Ignatius M. Karma?" Hal questioned.

"Yes it is, how can I help you?" Said the voice.

"No sir, its how I can help you!" Hal said enthusiastically. "You see, Mr. Karma, a mutual acquaintance suggested I call you regarding a rather lucrative investment opportunity." Hal continued.

"Lucrative you say?" Asked the voice with guarded enthusiasm. "Why that's my favorite kind of investment." He continued.

"I'm glad to hear you say that sir, because this one has got nothing but upside." Hal said emphatically.

"And who did you say referred you to me?" asked the voice.

Hal was used to this and often mumbled a first name and pronounced a common last name distinctly. He didn't know any of the people he called but he did know that it is human nature to fill in pauses or unintelligible information with familiar information. Hal knew almost everyone knew someone with a common last name. He knew that most people naturally filled in the blank left by the mumbled first name with the name of the person they knew that had the common last name. This allowed Hal to make it seem as if he was referred by a trusted friend of the stranger he was calling.

"Mumblebulbr Johnson." Hal replied.

"No, sorry, I don't actually know anyone whose last name is Johnson." Replied the voice.

"Achoo (sneezing) Jackson". Responded Hal.

"Donahue Jackson…oh, you mean Don Jackson?" Replied the voice.

"Yes sir!" said Hal. "The one and only."

"Why I haven't heard from him in years!" shouted the voice with glee. "Of course I didn't know his father, let alone that his father's name was John but if he referred you, I guess you're okay." He continued.

Hal proceeded in telling Karma about the Cacamente Gold Mine of Peru. He told him that it was the richest new discovery of gold in the past 50 years and that it often paid five dollars to one in the first three months and that after three months he could either choose to re-invest or take cash out; it was up to him.

"Sounds like a good deal." Said the voice.

"Very good sir." Hal said. "How much can I put you down for?" He asked.

"Is this the only good investment opportunity you have?" asked the voice.

"No sir, I have many others." Replied Hal

"How many others?" Queried the voice.

Hal paused for a moment. He thought to himself, should he name all 10 of his bank accounts as investments.

"I have nine others." Hal replied.

"Then here's what I'll do." Said the voice. "I'll wire a token amount, say $100 into each of the accounts attributed to those investments. Then, if the money goes through, I'll wire an additional $50,000 into each of the accounts within 48 hours." He continued.

"But why do you need each account, can't you just wire it all to one account?" Asked Hal.

"Forgive me young man, but I have developed this way of doing business because I have been burned before." Said the voice. "I am a shut in and have to do all of my business over the phone." He continued.

Hal thought a moment. Should he give this guy all of his account numbers? He knew it was against his better nature but the half a million dollar payday was too tempting, especially when he was grooving off the mojo of a hot streak. Hal got out the little black book where he kept all of his bank account numbers and, one by one, read them over the phone. After he read the last number the line was disconnected. Hal called back but the line was busy. Karma was obviously depositing the money. He went to lunch.

Hal checked all ten of his bank accounts when he returned from lunch and found each one had a deposit of $100. He called Karma back to tell him that the money went through but there was no answer. Hal decided to take the rest of the day off. After all, it was 2:00 P.M. on a Friday and he had a pretty good day. He wondered if Karma would come through with the $500,000 as promised on Monday but even if he didn't he still had an extra $100 in each of his bank accounts. Chump change for him, true, but it still could pay some bills. It was a rainy weekend in Manhattan. Hal spent it snuggling up to a good book. He shunned the usual party scene and decided to relax.

Monday morning, Hal went online to see if Mr. Karma's $500,000 had been deposited into his accounts. He checked the Cacamente account. There was only $100! He checked each of the other accounts. All of them had the same amount, $100! It was as if the $100 deposited by Karma had eaten all of his money. Hal knew that was impossible. It was more likely that Karma had stolen it through wire transfers but Hal knew that all he had to do was trace the IP address to where the money was transferred and he could get a hacker "acquaintance" of his to get it back.

Hal called all ten banks. He asked each of them to trace who withdrew the money that was in his accounts as of last Friday morning. Each of them told him it was withdrawn by him. When Hal asked each of them to trace the IP address the money was sent to every one of them give him his own IP address. Hal was home alone all weekend. His computer was shut off and unplugged the whole time. He knew that it was physically impossible for the money to have been wired to his computer. Irate, Hal dialed Mr. Karma. The phone rang several times. Then the line picked up.

"Hillside Cemetery, Bill Peterson" Said the voice on the other end.

"I want to speak with Mr. Karma!" Hal demanded.

"There's no one here by that name." Replied Peterson.

Hal bit his lip, trying to hold back his anger enough to make a calm, rational response to Peterson.

"Listen to me, please." Hal said. "Two days ago I called this number and spoke to a Mr. Ignatius M. Karma. I am in no mood for a prank!"

"No sir." Said Peterson. This is an actual cemetery in New Orleans and we've had this same phone number for at least 20 years." He continued.

"Well how was I able to talk to Mr. Karma two days ago?" Said Hal in exasperation.

"Did you say two days ago?" Replied Peterson.

"Yes." Replied Hal.

"Why that's when our phone was out due to a downed phone line." Said Peterson.

"A downed phone line?" Replied Hal

"Yes, a phone line snapped and fell onto one of our graves but we found the problem and had it fixed before Saturday." Peterson said.

"Was the name on the grave Ignatius M. Karma?" Hal asked.

"No sir, it was Frank Mayhew." Replied Peterson.

A chill ran down Hal's spine as he quickly hung up the phone. That name rang a bell. Back when Hal first began scamming seniors, he used to leave them with $100 in their account. He thought is was bad luck to leave someone completely broke. He remembered Mayhew because Mayhew had 10 different bank accounts and when Hal cleaned him out he left $100 in each account. He read that Mayhew had committed suicide two days after he was swindled.

Hal knew that it was not just a man who had cannibalized his ill-gotten fortune. He understood the significance of the name used, Ignatius M. Karma, I.M. Karma which suddenly sounded like I Am Karma. He knew that Karma itself had caught up with him and repaid the misfortunes his scams had visited upon countless of society's most vulnerable citizens.

In his soul, Hal knew he would never see the money from his ten accounts. He knew that over the next few months he would have to stand helplessly by as one by one, his houses, apartments and cars would be foreclosed upon or repossessed. He knew instinctively that he had permanently lost his mojo and he would never be able to scam another senior. He knew the days of living well were over. He knew he would have to go back to being Harold and the best he could hope for was a life sentence in a crappy day job and a small apartment. Hal walked out onto his balcony, looked out over central park and jumped.

The Ghost Train

He boarded the train at Platt Junction. He walked past the weary people in drab clothing with blank looks on their faces. He found a window seat near the back of the car. He walked over to it and sat down.

He noticed a dank smell. At first he couldn't place it but he knew that he had smelled it before. Then he figured it out. It was a mixture of blood, sweat and tears soaked into the seats over time and baked in by the hot sun. He reached up to the top of the sliding window hoping to open it and introduce some fresh air but the window wouldn't budge.

As the train pulled away from the station, he resigned himself to looking out the window and regulating his breathing to avoid the nose curling stench of the seats. He let his mind wander. He thought about his lovely, young wife. He missed her terribly even though he just left her less than an hour before. That hour seemed like a century. He guessed that was just a consequence of being in love, time apart seemed like an eternity.

He was on his way to work but he couldn't remember specifically what he was supposed to be doing that day. Working in a mine, like he did, there were basically only two jobs, digging or removing dirt. Everyday he was either doing one or the other. He couldn't remember which he was doing today. Perhaps he was still half asleep. He knew he should have had a cup of coffee before he left the house but he was running late.

He stared out the window for about a half an hour. There was nothing but scenery on the lonely stretch of track between Platt Junction and the mine he worked at. Then he saw another train approaching from the opposite direction. He couldn't recall, the last time he had seen a train on the opposite side of the tracks. For some reason, it made him recall a legend he once heard but he couldn't recall when he heard it.

It was The Legend of The Ghost Train. It was a train that had a bad accident. Its entire crew and all of its passengers were killed. It was said that it only appeared to trains that were about to have a bad accident. As the train on the opposite side of the tracks drew closer and closer he began to wonder if it could be "The Ghost Train".

First, the engine passed. The driver stared straight ahead but the fireman who stoked the engine began yelling when he saw them. Then, the first passenger car passed. The people on it began screaming. The people in his car turned to look at them. They all had blank stares on their faces. One little boy was an exception because he waved at them.

He wondered why the people on his train were so calm about the viewing of the train on the opposite track. Didn't they know that it was the ghost train? Was he the only one on his train that realized the danger they could possibly be in?

Then, as each passenger car passed, the people on the opposite train seemed visibly upset. By the last two cars, the train began rocking and as they got another 100 yards down the track, he heard the unmistakable sound of a train derailing. He heard the twisted, metallic moans of a dying train and the screams of passengers as he saw the caboose lurch to the right and fall off of the tracks.

He wondered if that was the Ghost Train of legend and if he witnessed the legendary accident that left so many people dead. Then, in one fluid motion, he and all of the other passengers in his car turned their heads and faced forward. His mind seemed strangely numb now. It was completely devoid of thought as their train kept chugging along over a gorge that was 1,000 feet deep over a track on a trestle that had collapsed 100 years before and disappeared into the mists of time.

The Soul Collector

On an excursion to an eco-forest in the Amazon, a group of tourists came upon a wild jaguar. The group, which consisted of a tour guide, an elderly couple and their nine year old grandson, and a middle aged man. The jaguar stood its ground, growling at a low pitch. The middle aged man puckered up his lips. A sound like the whistling wind came out of his mouth. The jaguar froze. The man calmly walked up to it and made the same whistling sound. He gently stroked the jaguar's furry head. Then he whispered.

"It's okay, you can leave."

With that, the jaguar turned and calmly walked away. Never turning back. The group stared in amazement.

"How did you do that?" The nine year old asked. "The whistling sound is the cry of the lost souls." He said. Every animal and every ghost understands it. When I whistled the cry of the lost souls, the jaguar knew I was beyond its reach and it had no choice but to obey me."

That night, the group made camp in the wilderness and by the light of a bonfire, the man told his story. He said that when he was five years old, he drowned in a pool. He awakened in a drawer in the hospital morgue. He said he still had scars on the bottom of his feet from kicking at the drawer with the bottom of his feet. I time, a worker overheard him and opened the drawer. He was sent back to the hospital and released to his parents the next day.

The next year he went to elementary school. His classes were in the dilapidated main building which was over 100 years old. During the first week there, he began to hear voices during class. At first he was afraid. Then he realized that the voices were giving him the answers to the questions his teacher was asking him.

As he grew up he attracted more and more ghosts. He was the only one who could see them and hear them. He didn't dare tell anyone about them because he knew they would think he was crazy. The ghosts hung around his classes, followed him down the street, and haunted his parent's house.

During his first year of in high school, he was hounded by a group of bullies. They spread rumors about him, threatened him, and kept on bugging him. One day, three of the bullies tried to extort money from him when they got him alone in the bathroom. Some of his ghosts turned off the lights and slammed the bullies around the bathroom. After that no one messed with him again.

When he was 21, he rented a small house. By then, the nearly 300 ghosts he attracted were haunting the house and yard. Other people began to see his ghosts as well. Neighbors noticed shadowy figures lurking about his backyard. They saw faces peeking out of his windows. They even saw strangely dressed people following behind him while he did his gardening in the front yard in broad daylight. The postman saw an elderly Native American following him and a neighbor saw him walk through an elegantly dressed woman in clothing from another time period.

One night, he heard a whistling sound. A wind filled his bedroom on a calm summer night. It permeated his dream and awakened him from a deep sleep.

He gasped and when he did, he felt a rush of air enter his body. No one ever saw ghosts around his house again. They were all inside of him.

He said he didn't feel them. They didn't haunt or control him. They were just there. Any time he passed by a cemetery, a hospital, or anywhere else a lost soul would be he would hear the whistling sound, feel the wind on his face, and take a deep breath.

One day, one of his friends called him. She told him she bought a condominium and found that it was haunted. He came over one day, heard the whistling wind, took a breath and the haunting stopped. That friend told another friend, who told another person who told someone else and before long, people were paying him to visit their house and take away their ghost problem. Within a year, he was making so much money solving people's ghost problems that he didn't need a job. Through his work, he was able to travel all over the world and see places he would have never been able to afford to go to.

One time, a woman hired him because her family members were being drained of their energy by something supernatural in their house. He sent the family away and spent the night in their house. About 3:00 A.M. he awoke and immediately felt a heaviness on his chest. It felt like someone was sitting on his chest. Although he couldn't see anything, he could feel a hand on each shoulder, holding him down. He felt his energy draining. As it drained, he began to see the shadowy figure of a woman on top of him.

He heard the whistling wind but it wasn't coming from the room, it was coming from inside of him. Then, he saw some mist leave his mouth, surround the shadowy figure and sweep it towards his face. He heard the shadowy figure scream in terror as the mist swept it into his nose. As with the other lost souls, he felt no ill effects with the intake of this lost soul.

A month later, he received a contract from a family that bought a farm in Nebraska. They were being haunted by the ghost of a previous owner who had murdered his entire family with an axe before hanging himself over 120 years before. The family reported lights going out constantly cupboards in the kitchen opening and closing rapidly, Dishes flying across the room and crashing against the wall, shattering into a thousand pieces. The children would wake up in the middle of the night to see a man with a bloody axe standing over their bed. Sometimes blood would drip onto them.

He arrived at the house in the early evening. The family was already in a hotel. He sat in the kitchen and turned the lights off. As night fell, plates began rattling in the cupboard. Then the cupboard doors opened and closed rapidly. As they did, plates and cups flew out of them, smashing against the opposite wall.

Then by the light of the moon shining from outside of the kitchen window, he saw the shadowy figure of a large man, with a beard, holding an axe standing at the threshold between the kitchen and the living room. The shadowy figure materialized into a full ghostly apparition. He began yelling.

"I know who you are and why you are here! This is my house! My House!" He yelled.

Then the evil ghost picked the axe up over his head and began to charge the soul collector. The soul collector issued the whistling wind from his lips. A mist quickly surrounded the ghost. He swung his axe at it but the mist shredded the ghost axe. The ghost tried to punch at the mist but the mist enveloped him and appeared to have him in a headlock. The soul collector could see the ghost still trying to grab at the mist with his hands but the mist had too much power. Within seconds the ghost was swept in anyway. It couldn't resist the combined power of 2,000 ghosts that now lived within the soul collector.

The soul collector said it was that particularly nasty ghost that made him realize two things. First, that he had the power to send the ghosts from inside his body towards something outside of his body. Second, that he could use the power of the ghost wind to benefit mankind.

Later that month, he moved into a small apartment in a crime ridden, gang infested section of a major urban city. As night fell, the regular people went inside their apartments, locked their doors, drew their blinds and turned off their lights. The criminal element came out and ruled the streets. He heard loud music, loud talking, arguments, people shouting and occasional gunshots all night long.

From his darkened apartment, he peered out from behind his blinds. He saw drug deals going down, addicts getting high and fighting in the streets. That first night, he resisted the temptation to release the ghost wind. He figured that this was an experiment and he needed to get a base line and see what a typical night on that street was like before he released the ghost wind.

The next night, began as the previous one had. Loud music, loud talking, arguments and fighting began almost immediately. He released the ghost wind at 10:00 p.m., almost immediately the loud music stopped. The arguments continued. Then he heard screaming. Then gunshots. Then the screeching of tires and cars speeding away. By 10:30p.m. the streets were quiet.

The following night, he released the ghost wind at 8:00 p.m. he heard gunshots, screams and cars speeding away. The streets were quiet by 8:15 p.m. The next night there was less noise but he released the ghost wind at 8:00 p.m. and the noise stopped immediately. By the sixth night the streets were calm and quiet. Nothing was seen or heard outside. After a week, the regular people began to come out of their apartments at night. After another week there was a robust civil nightlife on the street and not a criminal in sight. He succeeded in transforming a neighborhood without evicting the people who were in it!

For the next two years he moved from one major urban city to another spending no more than two weeks in each and totally transforming the neighborhoods he chose to stay in. No one knew why the neighborhoods had changed so drastically in a short period of time. There were stories told by criminals across the globe of neighborhoods that were haunted but regular people didn't believe them because they never experienced the hauntings. They just knew that their neighborhood changed.

Then one day, he read about a terrorist group kidnapping 400 teenage girls and holding them for ransom, threatening to sell them into slavery if the ransoms were not paid. The Soul Collector flew to a major city in that nation. He made it known that he had come to that nation to negotiate with the terrorists. Within a day or two he was kidnapped and taken to the location where the girls were being held. When the leader of the group asked that he produce proof that he was legitimate, the soul collector asked that he be untied. He got out his cell phone and dialed up a bank account and shoed the leader that in it was the exact amount the terrorists were asking for. The leader and his comrades around him seemed very pleased.

Some of them left and returned with a skinny man whom they called their accountant. The man produced a bank account number and routing instructions. Then their captive told them that he wasn't there to offer them the money they asked for, although he certainly had it. He was there to offer to spare their lives in exchange for the girls. The terrorists and their accountant laughed heartily. When they saw that their captive wasn't laughing, anger filled the eye of the leader. He whipped out a pistol and pointed it to the head of their captive.

"What's to prevent me from blowing your brains out right now and transferring the money myself?" He yelled.

"You don't know the password to release the money." The soul collector replied.

"Tell me the word, tell me now!" The leader demanded as he cocked the trigger of the pistol.

"It's not a word." The soul collector said. It's a sound." He continued slowly.

Then the soul collector puckered his lips and made the sound of the whistling wind, the ghost wind. A mist came pouring out of his mouth. It split into many fingers each grabbing a terrorist and entering their mouth. The terrorist began shooting but instead of shooting at their captive, the mist or the kidnapped girls, they shot each other.

Then, the soul collector opened his wallet, and pulled out a faded piece of newspaper. It showed a photo of him walking into a nearby town with 400 teenage girls. His audience couldn't believe their eyes or their ears. They heard some fantastic tales but were they real or fantasy? They went to bed that night with many questions.

The next morning, they awoke ready to hear some answers but the soul collector was gone. Their guide said he walked into the jungle to help a tribe nearby. He told the guide not to wait for him. In the months since their encounter, every time one of the people who were on the jungle trip with him read or hear about something good happening unexplainably they remember the soul collector and wonder if it was him.

Travels of My Soul

VERSE 1

You can't tell that I have traveled
By merely looking at me
But if you gaze into my eyes
Soon enough you will see
That I have traveled
Travels of my soul

VERSE 2

Not just from dusty desert
To the sparkling blue green sea
No, I have really traveled
The width and breadth of the galaxy

While others speak of tropical jungles
Or a lady whose skin is fair
I describe the plant Venus
And the picturesque scenery there
For I have traveled
Travels of my soul

VERSE 3

Some may simply doubt me
Others might ask me why
My only answer is a feeling
My soul is my reply

If by some chance the feeling grabs you
And you find yourself among the few
Your heart shall awaken to find the truth
And your soul will travel too

Travels of my soul

The Hell Banger

The Hell Banger is a two headed monster that has four eyes. One arm is shotgun and the other is a chain saw. He wears a black hoody. He has sharp teeth, white sox and black shorts. He's bald and has a tattoo in the shape of an evil clown. He has devil horns and long fingernails that are sharp like knives. He has wings like a bat and hooves. He skins the bodies of his victims and uses the skin to make paper for his novel. He decapitates victims and surrounds them with rubber to make soccer balls out of them. He has a British accent but he speaks Gibbersh.

The Story of Hell Banger

Payaso Demon was a gagster that got bitten by a Tasmanian devil that escaped from the L.A Zoo. The same day he was bitten by a rattlesnake. The rattlesnake venom mixed with the saliva of the Tasmanian devil and transformed him. He became a creature of monstrous features and an insane mind. He became a serial killer reaper. His first victim was a <u>grotesque</u> old lady who was walking down East Lake Street. He stopped in front of her. She yelled "you're ugly." Then he shot her in the foot and chain sawed her head off. He had a difficult time getting her soul out of her body because it had been encrusted there for over 90 years.

He said "Gaba Baba yay! I did it piznerlcal flook gah!" in his British accent. He was surprised when the lady came back to life long enough for her dead head to say. "You suck gangster scum!"

His next victim was from Northern Egypt. Syed Faboony was a probation officer who was always messing with Payaso. Syed was munching on Chili fries at Dinos when Payaso caught up with him.

Payaso decapitated him while he had a mouthful of Chili fries and shot him in the chest four times. He took Syed's soul and locked it in the bathroom at Lincoln Park, which hadn't been cleaned since 1942.

By the time Colonel Puffinstuff led the investigation into the Hell banger killing the mood in Lincoln Heights was frightening. People were afraid to walk down the street and Lincoln Park went out of business due to a haunted bathroom. Colonel Puffinstuff found an old book called "The Hell Bangers Guide to Cool Clothes and Killing Victims"

When he went to the crime scene for victim number three he brought the book. The crime scene was the merry go around at Lincoln Park. The third victim was Police officer in the gang unit. His body was strapped riding on a wooden horse and his head replaced the head of another horse. The fourth victim was a retired judge who locked up Payaso's dad in 1991. The wooden horse head was stuffed into his neck. His head was used to create an ant farm sand box.

Colonel Puffinstuff finally killed the hell banger when he cornered him buying pro club clothing at a swap meet. The colonel killed him by throwing a jar of nail polish remover on him while saying "Like a lotta dirt I'll rub you out." Payaso stumbled around for three minutes and then shriveled up like a dried out prune.

That was the last anyone ever heard from the Hell Banger. Yet his legend continues and people often tell his story, especially when Game of Thrones on hiatus or in reruns. Colonel Puffinstuff became a famous sleuth and wrote a series of novels that sold dozens of copies. Lincoln Park is still abandoned and late at night, if you listen very carefully you can hear the ghost of Syed Faboony yelling words that send chills down the spine of even the hardest Gangster... "I didn't even get to finish my Chili Fries!"

Life Lines

It began with a question. What if people only lived as long as the lines on the palm of their hand indicated they would? This was the question Hiram Bosworth attempted to answer in his doctoral dissertation.

A failed medical student and amateur parapsychologist, Hiram, or Ram to his friends, had not come up with this question lightly. It had been simmering inside of his mind for years. He remembered when he first encountered an inkling that life lines foretold one's life expectancy. He was nine years old and his mother and aunt went to a palm reader. The palm reader refused to read his aunt's palm. She just looked at it and flatly refused. The next day, his aunt was dead, a embolism exploded in her brain. She told her husband that she had a splitting headache. He went to the medicine chest in the bathroom to get her an aspirin and when he returned, moments later, she was dead.

A few days later, on a Saturday, Ram told his mother he was going to the park and rode his bicycle four miles to the house where the pam reader lived. He knocked on the door and when she answered he asked if she remembered him. When she indicated that she did, he asked her why she refused to read his aunt's palm. She told him she saw that her life line had reached its end.

When he was sixteen, Ram passed by a dead body at a crime scene. The body was lying face down and although a sheet was covering it, the right hand protruded from the sheet, palm up. He could see that the lifeline on the cadaver's hand was short. As he stared at the hand, a sudden gust of wind rushed past flipping open the part of the sheet that covered its head. He recognized the cadaver. It was a 19 year old gangster that he saw preying on other kids outside of his high school. His right eye was blown out along with the back of his head.

When he was in his early twenties, as a first year medical student, he interned at the local community hospital. He began looking at the palms of people who expired at the hospital. He began to notice that the lifelines of the old were long and the lifelines of the children and teens were short. Once, he even saw a baby who had died at birth. Its little palm had no lifeline at all.

After several years of interning at the hospital he was able to gage the length of the lifeline to the approximate age of the deceased. He knew which size meant a death in one's twenties, thirties, forties and fifties. By the time he was ready to write his dissertation, he had it down to a science. He could look at a cadaver's hand and, without looking at the body, know exactly how old the person was when they died.

In the middle of writing it, he wondered if he could use living people's lifelines to predict when they were going to die. He began looking at patients on his ward. He began to predict whether or not they would get better. He gathered evidence and found that in most cases he was accurate but not always. He was accurate enough that he could make money placing bets with other hospital staff. $20.00 here, $60.00 there, an occasional hundred dollar bill. The money added up and went a long way towards offsetting his medical school bills but there was a downside.

The thrill of gambling on lifelines consumed him. He made bets with staffers every chance he got. Most of the time he won. Sometimes he lost. It was the element of chance that attracted other people to bet against him and it was the element of chance that made betting on lifelines an addiction for him. In time, Ram let his studies lapse. He botched a few surgeries. He came onto the hospital administrator's radar. By the time he finished his dissertation, he was kicked out of the doctoral program for gambling on the job. He knew the State Medical Licensing Board would never issue him a license.

Despondent, Ram took to drinking. His student loans disappeared within a few weeks and he was evicted the small apartment he was renting. Being Homeless sobered Ram up quickly. He used his medical skills to treat sick and injured people in an alley behind a movie theater. He saved up money and within a month was able to live in a residential hotel near skid row.

Knowing that it would only be a matter of time before he was caught practicing medicine without a license, Ram transitioned away from that and signed up with a Temporary Employment Agency. Ram had skills as a typist and could file quickly and accurately. He went through a series of jobs at insurance companies, architectural firms, law offices and medical offices.

About a year after he began temping, he worked at a publishing company. He liked working there. One day, one of his bosses asked him if he could proof read a story they were thinking of including in about they were about to publish. When he finished proofreading the story, he was asked if he could proof read other things. He told them he could. They offered him a full time job as a proof reader with a substantial raise. It wasn't long before Ram moved out of the residential hotel and into a decent sized apartment.

Several months later, Ram got an idea. The dissertation he wrote might make a marketable book. After a few days, he got up the courage to ask his boss to look at it and see if he thought it might be something they would like to publish. His boss returned it to him a week later. He told Ram that in its present form it wasn't marketable but if he would dumb it down and make it interesting to the general population it might be something their company would publish.

Ram went home that night and began work on converting the dissertation into a book that might have popular appeal. First, he took out all of the medical terminology and academic language. Then, he removed the statistics graphs and charts. Finally he used sensationalized language and made plenty of exaggerated claims. He just needed to come up with a snappy title. Then it hit him. "How Your Lifeline Can Tell You How Long You Will Live!".

A week after his boss told him what to do Ram brought the finished manuscript to his office. His boss signed him to a publishing contract that same day. With his boss, the executive Vice President of the company behind it, "How Your Lifeline Can Tell You How Long You Will Live!" was in stores within a month. Ram was doing talk shows and book signings within a week of that. By the end of the year, the book was a best seller.

The Wet Woman on The Road

Billy and Bob were on their way up to their log cabin in the mountains. As they drove up the winding road they realized that they had to slow down as an early evening fog rolled in. They drove slowly and while they knew there was a full moon out, they couldn't see it as thicket after thicket of tall pine trees dotted the roadside. They couldn't see the moon but could hear a river rushing somewhere below them. Curve, after curve the pitch black road was illuminated by their car's headlights.

Then, as they rounded one particular bend, their headlights suddenly flashed upon a face. Bob slammed on his breaks. There, about 10 feet in front of their car was a pale white woman in a white evening gown. The gown, her hair and skin were wet. Billy got out of the car.

"What are you doing here?" He yelled.

"Help, you've gotta help me!" She replied frantically.

"What's wrong?" Billy asked.

"I must have fallen asleep at the wheel and went over the side of the road. My daughter is trapped in the car!" She replied.

"Hold on." said Bob. "We'll pull the car over and follow you to the car."

Bob drove the car a quarter a mile up the road and parked in a small turnoff. The two men walked over to the place where they first saw the woman but she wasn't there. They looked around and saw some skid marks about 50 yards from where they saw her. They began walking down a newly carved trail of broken branches and mowed down saplings. They could hear the river rushing below them. When they got to the bottom of the trail, they saw the river. It was illuminated by slivers of moonlight that filtered through some of the trees. It seemed about seven or eight feet deep and was traveling at a high rate of speed.

They could see impressions in the mud. They looked like something heavy had made them. This must be where the woman's car went into the river but where was the car? Then, they heard a loud voice yelling. "Over here!" It said. They looked about 25 yards downstream and saw a large object wedged between two boulders on the edge of the river. They knew it was metallic because of the eerie way glints of moonlight reflected off of its chrome.

Billy and Bob walked towards the object. As they got closer they could see it was a big, old car and that it was wedged at an angle, the passenger side was submerged beneath the water. The driver's side was right at water level. When they got even closer, they could see an arm and hand protruding from the driver's side window. It seemed to be waving them over. The voice was still yelling "Over here", but it seemed muffled.

When they arrived at the car, Billy climbed up on the large boulder on the passenger side and Bob climbed up on the boulder on the driver's side. Billy peered beneath the water and could immediately tell that the window on the passenger side door was broken open. There was nothing alive over there. Bob climbed onto a much small boulder, looked down onto the driver's side and couldn't believe his eyes.

The driver's side window was opened about 1/3 of the way. Inside the car, the mother was dead, her head submerged below the rushing water. One arm was holding an infant girl's head up to the inside roof inner lining of the car in a small air pocket, just inches above the rushing waters. The other arm was protruding out of the window, the rushing river water bobbing it up and down in a motion similar to someone motioning to come closer.

Bob called Billy over to his side. Billy quickly complied. Bob told Billy to reach his arms inside the opening and grab the infant girl. He did. Then bob got a large rock and smashed it against the car window. It shattered, sending pieces of glass towards the open car window on the passenger side. Just as the glass shattered, Billy yanked the infant girl out of the car. The air pocket the little girl was in quickly became submerged beneath the rushing waters.

The little girl was comatose but breathing. Bob figured she was likely suffering from hypothermia. Bob took off his jacket and wrapped the infant in it as he walked up the trail. He told Billy to run up to the car, get their cell phone and call 911. Within about 22 minutes a helicopter airlifted the infant to a hospital.

Billy and Bob were hailed a heroes. They met the infant's father and, although he was sad over the loss of his wife, he was grateful for the life of his daughter. Bob and Billy told their story to everyone who would listen. Some believed them. Some didn't. They themselves didn't really understand what they saw and heard but they did understand that there is nothing stronger than a mother's love because, as far as they were concerned, a mother's love reached from beyond the grip of death to save her child.

Monster Mosh

By Teacherz

Words and Melody By M. Wilkins, Music By D. Brewer, M. Nagaoka, P. Eberhardt

VERSE 1
Grading papers in my classroom
Late one night
My eyes beheld
A scary sight
The dissected frogs
Began to move
As the air conditioning whistled
An eerie tune

CHORUS
They did the mosh
The monster mosh
The mosh
The monster mosh

They did the mosh
The monster mosh
The monster mosh

And the whole school rocked

VERSE 2
Animated objects spread from
The science building east
To the faculty lounge
Where the cockroaches feast
The dust bunnies in the hall
Began swirling around
As the lockers banged
Along to the sound

(repeat chorus)

VERSE 3
Milk cartons started dancing
With cafeteria food
Scary sounds started coming
From the bathrooms
The whole place seemed haunted
But I didn't care
It was the most fun I had
Since I started working there

(repeat chorus, replace "they" with "we" in line 1)

The Dreaded Bungadun
of Blood Valley

Dark was the night that Mr. Jones led the twenty five brave British monster hunters marched down into desolate Blood Valley. Blood Valley was in the middle of the Gobi Desert 60 miles away from the nearest village.

Slippery was the path they marched along, Slippery from the fog that surrounded them. Dim was the light of the moon that lit the ground they tread upon. Grotesque was the face of the dreaded Northern Bungadun that threatened to rip open their stomachs and devour their liver and kidneys while they lay helpless screaming bloody murder.

Difficult was the journey as they began to march near the bottom of the narrow slope with hundreds of dagger like rocks jutting out, waiting for a victim to make a false turn or a false step and fall into them. Then it happened.

One of the monster hunters lost his footing and fell into a dagger rock. He stabbed his left thigh. Blood began pouring from the wound. Like sharks in the water, Bungaduns can smell blood in the air and three came running at the poor fellow from both sides. Another monster hunter rushed to help him.

One of the Bungaduns plucked off a dagger rock like it was a toothpick and stabbed the brave man through his right eye. The dagger rock went through his brain and out the back his skull. Then the Bungadun pulled the dagger rock out and ate the man's brain like it was a shish kabob, while the other two Bungaduns ripped open the cut man's stomach and began munching on his liver and kidneys.

The mood was tense as Mr. Jones and the other 23 British monster hunters scattered in groups of four. Six new Bungaduns gave chase and picked the monster hunters off one by one as they separated from their groups.

Then Mr. Jones was alone. Surrounded by all 9 Bungaduns!. He had to create a way to escape. He pulled out his pistol and shot wildly at the Bungaduns. They were unharmed. They stared at him menacingly, ready to pounce. Resigned to his fate, he took one last drag of his cigarette and blew out the smoke.

To his surprise, as the smoke touched one of the Bungaduns it caught on fire. It touched another one and that one caught on fire too. There were seven Bungadun not on fire. Six of them began running uphill. The two on fire chased after them One of the Bungaduns charged Mr. Jones. He took a deep drag on his cigarette and blew out a puff of smoke. The charging Bungadun caught on fire. Mr. Jones moved and it crashed into some dagger rocks and was stuck burning to death.

As he looked up the slope he could see the other Bungaduns running up the hill bursting into flames as well. He was the lone survivor of the journey and to this day, the only man to have killed a dreaded Bungadun.

Author Biography

Mark Wilkins

A Storyteller

My name is Mark Wilkins. I am best known to my readers as A Storyteller. I pen the A Storyteller Series of Books for Love Force International Publishing. Unlike most other book series, it does not concentrate on a particular character or a particular story line. Instead, it focuses on books of short stories in various genres by a particular author, namely myself. Some of the books in the A Storyteller Book Series include serious fiction (A Week's Worth of Fiction), humorous fiction (Slices of Life) and a mixture of serious and humorous fiction and non-fiction (Classroom Confessions) and supernatural Fiction (Stories of The Supernatural).

The readers who enjoy my books like reading that sparks their imagination. They like stories with memorable and quirky characters on unusual topics. They like unexpected twists and turns in the plot. If any of these things my readers enjoy describe you, then you too will enjoy my writing.

I am comfortable writing in many different genres. I write both humorous and serious fiction. Some of my stories are based on true events, others are totally my invention. It is up to you, the reader, to decide which stores are based on factual events and which are completely my invention because I'm not telling. I like to tell stories and I work very hard at making those stories both compelling and entertaining. I hope you enjoy reading my books.

.

Kindle Books by Love Force International Publishing

Whether you are interested in true stories, fiction, humor, action, adventure, spiritual insights, quotes, poetry, self-help or children's books, Love Force International has got you covered. **Our 99 cent commitment,** our commitment to a 99 cent price for all our kindle e book titles so that people around the globe can afford them, means there has never been a better time to stock up on Books published by Love Force International!

NOTE: Books with AINs are available now the others will be available soon. All Titles are printed in English. Books with an SP after the title also have a version translated into Spanish.

The Reader Series is a series of readers that are a sampling of writings by one or more authors.

The Prophet of Life Reader (7 Book Sampler) Volumes 1 & 2
What do essays, articles, stories, poetry and quotes have in common? They are all in this sampling of stories, poems and other writings from 7 of The Prophet of Life's writings found in these Kindle books.
Author: The Prophet of Life   **ISBN:** 978-1-936462-07-0
ASIN: B015D716C0 Vol 1   ASIN: B06XBSWKX8 Vol 2

The Mark Wilkins Reader 7 Book Sampler! Volumes 1 & 2
One story from seven books by Mark Wilkins. Whether its smart spouses, inquisitive fools, teachers, gangsters or ghosts these books give you a good sampling of stories by the man known throughout the world as A Storyteller. Within its pages you will find horror, humor and pathos.
 Author: Mark Wilkins   **ISBN:** 978-1-936462-38-4 **ASIN:** B01MU0Z51H **Volume 1**

The Love Force International Reader 7 Book Sampler! 4 Books in This Series
Whether you want fiction,, humor, children's stories, poetry or quotes these books have got all of those and more! A sampling of 7 different books by three authors offered in Kindle books published by Love Force International.
Edited by Evan Lovefire **ISBN: ASIN:** B06XBHD9RX
Vol 1, ASIN: B06XBMGLNK **Vol 2**

The Love Force International Sampler, Spanish Books Edition SP Volumes 1 & 2
These books contain a sampling of 7 different books by three authors translated into Spanish. The books translated include What Faith has Taught me, Controversy, True Stories of Inspiration & General interest and Quotes about God by The Prophet of Life, Stories of The Supernatural, Slices of Life How to Become The Person You've Always Wanted by Mark Wilkins and Classic Children's Stories You've Likely Never Heard, and my first & second books of stupid little fables by Dr. Goose.
Edited by C. Gomez **ISBN: ASIN:** B06XB3RJ2K **Vol 1,   ASIN: Vol 2**

The True Stories Series is a series of books which include true stories by The Prophet of Life.

True Stories!
A riveting collection of true stories. Whether you want to know about the toddler taken by a gator at a Disney Resort, an 18 year old who doesn't exist, which popular restaurant chain has a corporate mentality of public humiliation for its employees or an alarming new trend that could affect your household this book has got it all and they are all absolutely true!
Author: The Prophet of Life   **ISBN:** 978-1-936462-16-2
ASIN: B06XVSZSZ9

True Stories: Inspiration and General Interest
SP
What do cell phone addicts, George Orwell, birds, Paul McCartney, The Nobel Prize, Black Friday, Led Zeppelin, garbage, a pep talk, tipping, Steve Jobs, Shakespeare, inspirational thoughts and your mother have in common? They are in true stories in this book. True Stories of Inspiration & General Interest brings together stories and poems about celebrities, trends and everyday people. Sometimes surprising, always interesting, it will entertain you and give you something to think about at the same time.
Author: The Prophet of Life   **ISBN:** 978-1-936462-15-5
ASIN: B00TXWVNUC   **ASIN:** B01BBCKFZU
(Spanish Edition)

Controversy
SP

What do Caitlyn Jenner, Donald Trump, a cure for AIDS, Chinese hackers, Adolf Hitler and Global Warming have in common? They are all at the heart of a controversy and there are stories about them in this unique book that turns tabloid headlines inside out.
Author: The Prophet of Life   **ISBN:** 978-1-936462-19-3
ASIN: B016MWU8NS   ASIN: B01CRF3098 (Spanish Edition)

True Stories of Crime and Punishment
SP
This book of serious crime stories is ripped from headlines all over the globe. From the family that vanished, to the 11 year old girl killed in a fight over a boy, to the prisoner who hasn't eaten in 14 years, to the severed human head found near the famous Hollywood sign these stories ripped will astound you and give you pause to think.
Author: The Prophet of Life **ISBN:** 978-1-936462-17-9
ASIN: B01406YZBE ASIN: B01N10ND7S (Spanish Edition)

Strange but True!

A collection of facts and stories about people, places and things that are strange and seem like fiction but are absolutely true!

Author: Mark Wilkins **ISBN: ASIN:**

The A Storyteller Series is a unique book series. Instead of concentrating on a particular character or genre, the series consists of collections of short stories by Author Mark Wilkins, Also Known As A Storyteller.

Slices of Life Volume 1
SP
is a collection of humorous short stories about life. Most of them deal with marriage and family members. From smart spouses to intelligent little children to guys trying to impress their friends and in-laws trying to master technology each story is like a little slice of life but together, they make up an irresistible pie. Sit back, grab a cup of coffee and enjoy some slices of lie because, before you know it, you will have finished the whole thing. **Author:** Mark Wilkins **ISBN:** 978-1-936462-11-7 **ASIN: B014ZF5VY0   ASIN: B01BBBZUL0 (Spanish Edition)**

Slices of Life Volume 2
SP
This sequel to Slices of Life has more humorous stories about the rich, the poor and the middle class. It even has a story about one of their pets. Ignorance is the main theme of this book, ignorance that has consequences that are sometimes touching but always humorous. So brew so coffee or tea, sit down and relax and enjoy another satisfying batch of more slice of life because, before you know it, you will have devoured the whole thing.

Author: Mark Wilkins **ISBN:** 978-1-936462-12-4 **ASIN:** B01M2B3YZ1 **ASIN:** B06XKP5C66   (Spanish Edition)

Stories of The Supernatural Volume 1
SP
Ghosts, demonic creatures, and Death. This collection of Short Stories will haunt and entertain you. Whether it's the classic evil of A Lump of Coal or the whimsy of A Ghost in the House this collection of Short Stories and poems will haunt, thrill and entertain you.
Author: Mark Wilkins **ISBN:** 978-1-936462-18-6
ASIN: B01M1N1QR5   **ASIN:** B01MA12YXY
(Spanish Edition)

Stories of The Supernatural Volume 2
SP
In this sequel to Stories of The Supernatural there are more Ghosts, Demonic Creatures and Death. This collection of short stories Centers of Ghosts and Monsters. Within its pages you will marvel at the exploits of The Soul Collector, Shudder at the mention of the dreaded Bungadun and of the Hell Banger and ride the rails on the ghost train. Strap on your seat belts, its going to be a bumpy ride! **Author:** Mark Wilkins **ISBN:** 978-1-936462-26-1
ASIN: B01MDJMSUY   **ASIN:**
   B01M4FXDL1   **(Spanish Edition)**

A Week's Worth of Fiction: Volume 1
SP
7 unusual stories of fiction that explores different sides of the genre. From what is going through the mind of a suicide bomber to a teacher on the edge sanity to an everyman who becomes a hero through senseless violence a journey of dark adventures awaits you.
Author: Mark Wilkins   **ISBN:** 978-1-936462-13-1
ASIN: B01521SQ02   ASIN: B06XVD21PM (Spanish Edition)

A Week's Worth of Fiction Volume 2
SP
From a girl battling a corporation over the rights to her blood to people engaging in life and death struggles this sequel to A Week's Worth of Fiction gives you 7 more stories that will thrill you, surprise you and make you think. Often dystopic and sometimes surreal, if you want stories you will never forget you only need to count to 7.
Author: Mark Wilkins **ISBN:** 978-1-936462-14-8
ASIN: B01LX9RZH7 ASIN: (Spanish Edition)

A Week's Worth of Fiction Volume 3
SP

From a woman trying to find love before her looks fade to a sky marshal struggling with racism to how Karma affects the life of a sanitation worker, this sequel to A Week's Worth of Fiction gives you 7 more stories that will thrill you, surprise you and make you think. Often dystopic and sometimes surreal, if you want stories you will never forget you only need to count to 7.
Author: Mark Wilkins   **ISBN:**   **ASIN:**
     ASIN: **(Spanish Edition)**

A Week's Worth of Fiction Volume 4
SP
From a soldier trying to solve a mystery to an indigenous man fighting barbaric tribal customs to a study of good and evil with a surprise outcome this sequel to A Week's Worth of Fiction gives you 7 more stories that will thrill you, surprise you and make you think. Often dystopic and sometimes surreal, if you want stories you will never forget you only need to count to 7.
Author: Mark Wilkins   **ISBN:**   **ASIN:**
ASIN: **(Spanish Edition)**

Classroom Confessions Volume 1
        SP
is a series of true stories from the front lines of public
education. Within its pages you will meet quirky
characters, the good, the bad and the over caffeinated.
Some of them are teachers, some students and some are
administrators. Some will make you laugh, others will
make you cry but they all play an important role in public
education. Their stories are written in way that will
entertain you and give you something to think about.
Author: Mark Wilkins **ISBN**: 978-1-936462-08-7
**ASIN: B00VNFJBX8   ASIN: B01MSV4N92
(Spanish Edition)**

Classroom Confessions Volume 2
        SP

 Is another series of true stories from the front lines of
public education. Within its pages you will meet
unforgettable characters like the French Substitute, Mr.
Happyhands, Harry Winkwater, The Bushwhacker and of
course, Julian. Some will touch your heart, others will give
you something to think about but they will all entertain
you. **Author:** Mark Wilkins   **ASIN: B01N1OCRVC
ASIN: B06XC9HDQV (Spanish Edition)**

The Love Force Novella Series: These are short novels of
varying length.

Karma: The story of one man who negotiates between two different cultures, and opposing life views competing for his attention. His conflicts and struggles are overshadowed by cosmic forces he cannot understand. Karma provides insights into the struggles and conflicts we all face.
Author: Mark Wilkins

ASIN: B0722R448R   ASIN: (Spanish Edition)

Coming Soon!!!!! Love Force International Paperbacks! Paperback duos (2 books in 1) and Trilogies (3 books in 1).

The Beyond Faith Series

Is a series of books that look at life from a spiritual perspective. No matter what your faith, you will find spiritual insights in these books that will enrich your life.

What Faith Has Taught Me
SP
I am just an ordinary person who has been privileged to have a life filled with miracles and revelations. There are many times when I had nothing except faith but faith was all I needed to sustain me. My faith and my God have taught me many life lessons. This book shares some of the things my faith has taught me and the spiritual insights I have gained because of my faith.
Author: The Prophet of Life   **ISBN: 978-1-936462-03-2**
ASIN: B01527IKT8   ASIN: B01EE3QSW2
(Spanish Edition)

Finding God in A Chaotic World
The world can seem so chaotic these days. Many people long for guidance. Many others want to get closer to God. How do you find God amidst the chaos and confusion? How can you discern God's messages from the multi-media blitz we are each bombarded with every day? Some people are part of an organized religion. Others are spiritual without a particular religion. Some are still searching, All of them trying to find God.

In this book, you will learn that The Lord communicates with how The Lord communicates with you. You will learn about the True Nature of God and realize just how profound God's Love and reach are. You will learn the secret of why God's will always prevails. If you are ready for revelations that may change the way you look at life in general and your life in particular, read this book.
Author: The Prophet of Life **ISBN:** 978-1-936462-01-8 **ASIN:** B00SLLZAAU

Finding God without Religion
People of faith are not exclusive to religion. There are many who are spiritual or agnostic. They don't fit into the doctrine, rituals and congregational community of religion. In this wisdom filled volume, people of faith but without an organized religion can gain insights into life, the afterlife and God without being brow beaten or guilt tripped into conversion. This volume is Book 2 of the Revelations of 2012 Beyond Faith series. Part 1 is entitled Finding God in A Chaotic World.
Author: The Prophet of Life **ISBN:** 978-1-936462-10-0 **ASIN:** B00XKPD86K

Inspiration For All 1
           SP
Selected Inspirational Writings. Whether you are of faith or just in need of inspiration in your life, this book full of inspirational stories, poems and essays will sustain and strengthen you on your journey. **Authors: The Prophet of Life & Mark Wilkins ASIN: B071ZM17V6**

Inspiration for All 2
           SP

This is a book of selected inspirational writings by three different authors. It will not only entertain you but will also stimulate your mind by offering you alternative ways of looking at things and opportunities to gain insights.
Authors: Mark Wilkins, The Prophet of Life & Dr. Goose.
ASIN: B0736JH6M9   Spanish **ASIN:** B072WK9JBH

Outrageous Humor Series
Books of stories and fake news articles for those with an
off-beat sense of humor.

Outrageous Stories
This book is filled with offbeat humor articles. All of them
are fictitious and many of them completely outrageous. No
one is safe from being made fun of be they terrorists,
Presidents, Dictators, The Movie and Record Business or
couch potatoes. If you are college age or older and have an
offbeat, irreverent, sense of humor, this book is for you!
Author: Mark Wilkins **ISBN:** 978-1-936462-33-9 **ASIN:**
B01LY3VZJR

More Outrageous Stories
This book is filled with more offbeat humor articles. All of
them are fictitious and many of them completely
outrageous. No one is safe from being made fun of be they
terrorists, Racists, National Holidays or the medical
establishment. If you are college age or older and have an
offbeat, irreverent, sense of humor, this book is for you!
Author: Mark Wilkins **ISBN:** 978-1-936462-33-9 **ASIN:**

Self Help Series
This consists of books by different authors designed to
help people improve their lives.

**Becoming The Person You've Always Wanted to Be
SP**

This self-help book offers a simple, yet profound method of making positive changes in your life. It includes a link to download exclusive, helpful companion worksheets to help you become the person you have always wanted to be.
Author: Mark Wilkins **ISBN:** 978-1-936462-39-1 **ASIN:**
　　　　　　　　ASIN: B01MSYVU6R (Spanish Edition)

Life Success Kit
Spiritual Thought Leader The Prophet of Life helps you clarify what success really means to you through a series of inspirational life lessons designed to give you new perspectives on achieving success and a blueprint for making changes in the things that are preventing you from becoming a success.
Author: The Prophet of Life　　　**ISBN:**　**ASIN:**

The Your Life in Rhyme Poetry Series
Is a series of Poetry books unlike any you have ever read whether it is an exploration of life itself through a thematic chapter on each of the various stages of life as in Reflections in The Mirror of Life, The mixture of thought provoking essays and inspirational poetry of Black in America or the exploration of a single topic as in Romance Returns or Life in Verse. The books in this series will have you rediscovering poetry in a way that will make you wonder why you ever avoided it in the first place.

Reflections in the Mirror of Life This unique book explores life through its harsh realities, pleasant diversions and positive possibilities. The book looks at modern society, the problems it faces, and the people who are a part of it. In a unique twist that's different from most books of poetry, Reflections is divided into five chapters, each of which explores a different theme woven into the fabric of modern life. The tone for each chapter is set by a free verse poem which is followed by a series of rhyming poems on that theme.
Author: The Prophet of Life **ISBN:** 978-1-936462-04-9
ASIN: B00V2TSAXC

Black in America is an exploration of racism through essays and poems. It spans from the beginnings of the Civil Rights movement through today. It includes a powerful new poem "Baltimore" and a perspective on the church shooting in South Carolina. It looks at people who have been lightning rods for race relations in America and has some surprising insights into the people and events that have shaped race relations in America for the past 60 years. Issued on the 50th anniversary of the March on Selma (1965), this book is a good companion for anyone who wants to gain insight into the Civil Rights movement, race relations and racism itself.
Author: The Prophet of Life   **ISBN**: 978-1-936462-09-4
ASIN: B00S05QSXA

Every Lyric Tells A Story   A collection of unique song lyrics that tell compelling stories about people, their lives, their hopes and dreams. You can find yourself and people you know in many of them.
Author: The Prophet of Life & Mark Wilkins   **ISBN**:
ASIN: B01NAFDWZW

Romance Lives A Collections of romantic love poems. It is divided into three sections. The Hunger about the need for love we all have, the romance about courtship ritual of romancing it takes to create a lasting in the one you choose and the deep emotions involved in making love a lasting love.   **Author: The Prophet of Life   ISBN: ASIN:**

Life in Verse

A collection of poems about life. The poems and song lyrics are about people, their lives, their hopes and dreams. You can find yourself and people you know in many of them. **Author:** The Prophet of Life **ISBN**: **ASIN:**

The Best Quotes quotation series

Is a series of books filled with quotes attributed to the Prophet of Life whose quotes have been used by charities, corporations, institutions of Medicine and higher learning. The book includes a license to use any of the quotes as long as they are attributed to The Prophet of Life.

The Best Quotes About God   SP

This short book is filled with some of the more popular quotes about God attributed to The Prophet of Life. It is both thought provoking and inspirational. It is filled with dozens of quotes about God that one can read and copy for personal use.
Author: The Prophet of Life **ISBN:** 978-1-936462-20-9 **ASIN:** B018P0M8OC **ASIN: B01BJXYHLY (Spanish Edition)**

The Best Quotes on General Subjects

This short book is filled with some of the more popular quotes on general subjects attributed to The Prophet of Life. The book includes quotes on topics such as life, love, happiness, crime and punishment, wellness and includes many of the humorous quotes attributed to The Prophet of Life. You will find the wit and wisdom in its pages thought provoking and inspirational. It is filled with dozens of quotes about God that one can read and copy for personal use.

Author: The Prophet of Life **ISBN**: **ASIN:** B01M58L9LW

The Best Spiritual Quotes

This book is filled with some of the more popular quotes on Spiritual Subjects attributed to The Prophet of Life. Included are quotes on faith, mercy, life lessons, humanity and spirituality. You should find them to be profound, thought provoking and inspirational. It is filled with many pages of quotes that one can read and copy for personal use.

Author: The Prophet of Life **ISBN**: **ASIN:**

Children Storybook Series
All books are by Dr. Goose who writes in both prose and rhyming verse.

Classic Children's Stories You've Likely Never Heard SP
Help develop your child's creative abilities and develop their imagination by reading them stories from this book that has no illustrations. Whether it's a story about Prince trying to find the answer to a question, a spider talking about a savior, a kingdom in trouble or a child trying to save the world you will find yourself wanting to read these children's stories with international flavor again and again. This first book in the series is for smaller children.
Author: Dr. Goose **ISBN: 978-1-936462-40-7 ASIN:** B01NAF8QNU **ASIN: B01MR5PR84 (Spanish Edition)**

More Classic Children's Stories You've Likely Never Heard   SP
This sequel gives you more unknown classics. The book introduces new characters like a little chicken whose life is similar to a person's and a ballad about a hairy man. There is a story about a prince whose refusal causes an international incident. There is even an updated version of classic children's story everyone knows from different character's points of view. This second book in the series helps tweens and juvenile children creative abilities and develop their imagination as stories from this book that has no illustrations either.
Author: Dr. Goose **ISBN: 978-1-936462-41-4 ASIN:**
                     ASIN: (Spanish Edition)

My First Book of Stupid Little Fables   **SP**
Whether the greed of mooches and lunch thieves, sadistic
children, or bizarre stories about pets this first installment
in the series of irreverently humorous stories with twisted
endings about the selfish and the greedy delivers. It even
has the stupid little drawings! For Juveniles.
Author: Dr. Goose   **ISBN:** 978-1-936462-44-5 **ASIN:**
        ASIN: **(Spanish Edition)**

My Second Book of Stupid Little Fables   **SP**
Whether it's well-meaning but incompetent grandmas,
egotistical women, sadistic children, or crazy people in
shopping centers, this second installment in the series of
irreverently humorous stories with twisted endings about
the selfish and the greedy delivers. It even has the
drawings you love to make fun of just like the first one!
For Juveniles.
Author: Dr. Goose   **ISBN:**   **ASIN:**
        ASIN: **(Spanish Edition)**

More Children's Stories
School Kidz Volume 1 Elementary and Middle School SP
Six funny stories about kids who are smarter than their age. Within its pages you will meet A boy whose vocabulary is better than the adults in his school, a kid who escapes a spanking, A kid who gets a new cell phone with a built in problem and a brother and sister who learn how get rid of junk from an old aunt. Recommended for kidz ages 12-16. **Author: Mark Wilkins ASIN: B0717B6SQ4**

School Kidz Volume 2 High School   SP
9 stories about kids who are in high school. Within its pages you will meet a group of Kidz who get involved in a rotten egg war, a girl who doesn't exist, and a kid who sends a friend on a date with his sister. Recommended for kidz ages 14-18. **Author: Mark Wilkins ASIN: B071W5WZZN**

Coming Soon E Workbooks and an E Textbook!
A series of mini and one comprehensive E Textbook Under the title of Mr. Wilkins Teaches English by Mark Wilkins

The specific mini textbooks will be on topics such as Reading and Responding to Literature, and Methods for Writing Paragraphs and Essays. The Comprehensive text will include a weekly spelling component and both the mini texts and comprehensive Text will include creative lessons that promote creativity and critical thinking in students while fitting into common core standards. The mini texts will be no more than 99 cents each and the comprehensive text will be paperback for under $10! All of the books are freshly created and contain exclusive intellectual property you won't find in any other texts. These books are perfect for students learning high school English levels 9 & 10 whether you are a classroom teacher or are home schooling your child. We are making the commitment to keep all of the books at low prices to allow parents and school districts to afford texts in the face of shrinking educational budgets. Purchasers will be given an opportunity to receive an email with a printable version of the exercises and assignments as well as links to online testing free of charge.

Author: Mark Wilkins   **ISBN:**   **ASIN:**

Compelling Stories for Adaptation to Short Film
For Film Students

Compelling stories in a set location with six or less characters. Easily adaptable to screenplay with notes on adapting them.

Author: Mark Wilkins   **ISBN:**   **ASIN:**

www.ingramcontent.com/pod-product-compliance
Lightning Source LLC
Chambersburg PA
CBHW030547130626
46552CB00006B/2466